THERE WAS A TIME...

Anne Carroll

Drawings by

Laabs Graphics

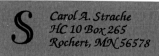

Carol A. Strache
HC 10 Box 265
Rochert, MN 56578

First Printing, June, 1992

**To Bill and Nelaina
and the all-free people.**

TABLE OF CONTENTS

PREFACE

"Eternal vigilance is the price of liberty."
Wendell Phillips

The character of a nation is determined by its moral code. In the all-free nation, a Higher Power had determined the rules that would enable the people to live in harmony.

Now, the end of a time had come and it was the beginning of another.

There is an imaginary line drawn somewhere between freedom and tyranny. *Is it the natural order of events to go from one to the other or is there a way to protect freedom in a society?*

It is up to a society to evaluate whether bigger is always better.

When any group of people assumes more influence, they also have more power. With this power comes control, and along with this control comes responsibility of action. Guidelines must be drawn up and followed.

In the all-free society, many of these groups, with their power, influenced decision making. These groups had their own interests at heart and not the good of their country. Since these groups had so much money and influence, some wondered if society could help but be controlled by them.

Would its freedoms finally undo their society? Could freedom be given such a wide berth that there would be law and no order? Could too many laws create chaos?

All societies need a governing body to keep order, but it is up to the citizens in a free society to keep the government accountable for its actions. When the mainstream of society becomes complacent in its own life, and does nothing to nurture or protect what is best for society as a whole, that nation will disintegrate.

Would the all-free nation halt this disintegration from within or would a dictator somewhere decide the fate of the all-free nation?

CHAPTER I - IMMORALITY

There had been a time when the morals of the all-free people were heading in the same direction. They had a Higher Power who had given them standards to live by. Most people followed these standards. It was like a law to follow. Even their country, because of the people, wanted to follow these rules because everyone benefited.

Looking back it is difficult, even now, to say exactly when everything began falling apart. But slowly it did—at least at first. It seemed like there were so many reasons. *What caused this moral decay?* It was like all wrong began to be all right. People were arguing, trying to make sure their way was the one to believe in.

It seemed, for many years, the male and female all-free people tried to form families. They had children and were supposed to teach these children the standards to live by. But slowly, as more and more people began to intertwine, these families began falling apart. There were many more contacts among people and this created a dilemma.

A person could be "happy" or they could honor their commitment to each other. It wasn't very many years before it became common to have only one parent or a different set of parents to teach these children.

There had been a male and female of this species of people. In years past, the Higher Power had set down a special law. It was mostly followed. Of course no law was followed by everyone. It seemed that male and female were supposed to be together. In this way, they created children.

In the latter years, there were different interpretations of these rules and that was when many changes took place. At first, men who were infatuated with other men lived quietly. Their behavior was unacceptable in the all-free nation. The people, for the most part, were trying to follow the standards of the Higher Power. Their standards had kept them unified for many years. Now there were arguments. Men could live with men—women with women. There were no limits on practicing sexual immorality. *"Never mind the children, these practices wouldn't influence them,"* they said. Everyone began following their passion. There were no restraints. *Or were there?*

There had been so many advances in technology that it was no problem creating a life—even artificially.

Looking back at the times, there were warnings of these "unacceptable" practices. Oh, it was fun for awhile. Even male and female participated. No one cared who they were with. It was the best of times. *Or was it?*

It began slowly. The physical problems began to emerge. They had never seen anything like it before. It wasn't their fault that this Affliction started.

When the standards had been followed, people mostly had one partner. With this one partner, they solidified their union. They kept their physical commitment for each other. The Affliction couldn't be passed on. *Or had it even started?* No one knew how it came to be.

But they knew when it appeared. Slowly, like a ghost, the Affliction crept into their lives. Surely it wasn't their lifestyle. *What did it matter to anyone else how many partners they had, or the manner in which they practiced their physical commitment?*

Men and women were no longer made to be together. The old standards were not modern enough to be followed. Oh sure, there were some old fashioned people who hung onto the old ways. But every day they were bombarded with this alternate life style. "It was as right as the one they practiced," many said. The moral decay continued—fragmenting society.

Openly members of the same sex lived together. In years past, if members of the same sex lived together, everyone assumed they were "just friends."

No one needed to know their sexual preferences and therefore it did not affect anyone else. This was a way to be together but not affect the rest of society, despite rules which had been set down since the beginning of time.

But in the latter days, many people wanted these rules changed. They wanted to live together to openly show their affection for one another. Now, even the children were affected by this lifestyle. In years past only the older people knew this practice existed. *Why shouldn't everyone have been allowed to live together openly, as they chose to do? Why shouldn't the laws have been changed to accommodate this practice?*

Could it have been because if it were done secretly, it didn't affect anyone else? At least the children wouldn't know and everyone else could only guess. Others didn't care, as long as it didn't affect their lives.

Children knew a family as a mom and dad. The Higher Power had said years ago that this was the way to live to keep society unified.

So, why was there no restraint in individuals in those latter days?

Why did these people have to act on their passion? Could this society exist for long if the long-practiced rules were ignored or changed?

There were reasons for rules and when they were changed to accommodate some, would it be long before no rule was followed? Or was this a way to live? Were the old laws impractical?

In the beginning of time, it was said, when earth was formed—male and female were made for each other...made to have children.

"Did society have the right to change this?", some wondered. *Just because technology had come so far as to create children without this union, did people have the right to change the rules? Even if a male or female could have sex with the same sex, did that make it right?*

This free society was in the midst of all these questions when the Affliction began. No one guessed at that time just how all-encompassing it would be. They knew they had no cure. *But how was it passed on?* Many members of society had to die before the all-free people had any answers. Surely it couldn't have anything to do with their sexual practices. They had had many partners for years, never knowing even who they were. The men, especially, had made up their minds many years ago to act on their passion outside of their marriage. This was a common practice.

Then men with men, many partners, whom did it hurt? Never mind the physical reality that man was not made to accommodate another man. They had figured out how, even if it went against nature. *Did this have anything to do with the Affliction?*

It then became known that this Affliction lived in the flowing life source of their body and was spread in this sexual manner. It was also discovered that if something was used to protect them from this flowing life source, they could continue with many partners and practices.

Would this Affliction have even had a chance to get started if the old laws had been followed? Maybe these laws had a reason behind them. When they found a cure for the Affliction, would everything be carefree again? Would new laws be made? Could a society exist when people went against nature?

The all-free people would know the answers to these questions.

The forefathers of the all-free nation had set down basic rules for the all-free nation to follow. These rules were founded on religious principles even though they separated church and state. This separation was necessary so neither group would control the other but they could influence each other.

This was necessary so people would be able to worship in the way they felt best. Government would determine the rules to keep order in their society. This separation maintained a balance. Because of this separation, no religious group could dominate the control of the government and government was protected from domination by any person or group because officials were chosen by election of the people.

Government was instituted by the Higher Power and therefore, His laws should have been obeyed over the laws of men. When people lived in a morally correct manner, these laws of the Higher Power and man were not in conflict. The separation between church and state made it clear that government had no control over the church and therefore could not interfere with religious beliefs or teachings. In the latter days, many tried to say that the church should have no influence over the government. People wanted to take every reference of religion out of public life.

Immoral behavior began to be the correct way. No challenge could be made to the immoral life but wholesome religious teachings could be ignored or challenged.

Some government officials became corrupt. Laws were broadened to include all kinds of behavior that earlier were forbidden.

Regions within the all-free nation had their own laws and these laws, when challenged by the National Government, mostly were changed in the name of freedom. Because of this, the whole of society suffered.

Even many churches gave in to pressure to include people with immoral behavior. This could have worked for the good of society if these people would have accepted the teachings of the Higher Power taught in these churches, but they wanted these teachings to change for them.

There was a time when people read bedtime stories to their children. Children could play in their own yards, climb trees and walk to the park with their friends. This changed. There were fewer yards and trees and parents were afraid their children would be kidnapped in the park. They had no choice but to remain in their homes to be entertained by technology. In the latter years, technology brought violence into the home. Children watched this and were exposed to a part of life that robbed them of their childhood. What was more precious than a child; yet, society allowed this violence into the home. In a way, the all-free people had no choice. Society made them obligated to purchase all this technology, and many parents were too busy in their own lives to be aware of what their children were watching.

As technology increased, more of this violence entered. People were even able to purchase tapes to increase their sexual awareness. Such printed material was also available in an unlimited supply. People were becoming obsessed with only their own gratification. They were also setting impossible sexual standards for themselves, because they were trying to measure up to someone else's standards.

This impossible standard also led them to believe their partner didn't measure up. Constant exposure to more people and to all the material that was available made people discontent with what they had. Children, who always wanted their mom and dad to stay together, had no say in the matter. Their homes were broken while their parents searched for the perfect life.

CHAPTER II - BUSINESS

The Central Investors' Market was in an upward spiral. The rich were elated. They had never had so much wealth. Their motto was "Invest in the Central Investors' Market and be prepared for unprecedented growth." The investors' market was certainly an indication of how the wealthy were doing, but it was no longer a reliable measure of general economic conditions in the all-free nation.

Of course the poor had no money to invest and everything they earned had to be spent to live. A bigger gap between rich and poor was developing. It was subtle the way it happened.

There were many small plots of land covering the countryside. Most of the people supported their families from these divided lands. But it soon came about that to make more wealth, a person would need more land. At the same time, in the large cities, businesses were employing people at a greater wage than some could make on their own land. Therefore neighbors sold their plots to neighbors and moved to the cities. This resulted in larger plots, which meant they needed more and larger equipment.

Now there were businesses and factories to produce all the necessities and luxuries for an ever increasing population. This continued until greed took over.

The all-free businessman finally figured out that if he could make a profit paying workers in his own country, much more wealth could be made if he developed his business in all the underdeveloped countries, where workers were paid so much less.

The consumers were so busy buying that it didn't occur to them that more and more of what they purchased was not made in their own country. They didn't even notice that the prices (which should have been substantially reduced because of labor cost) were kept close to the price of items made in the free country. It didn't matter to anyone where anything was made. If someone wanted something and had a card to purchase it, they did. It hadn't been too many years before this that workers paid cash for most items they bought, or went without the item until they could afford it. What a wonderful invention, the card! Used instead of money, it unconditionally paved the way to more buying power. Everyone profited—*or did they?*

At the same time, the businessmen were busy selling raw materials obtained in the all-free nation to all these other countries so they could sell it back to the all-free nation as a finished product.

In some cases, the raw materials didn't even have to be taken inland of the other countries. They used ships as factories—made products, dumped the waste in the ocean and continued producing like clockwork, with all the financial aspects figured to the smallest detail. The all-free businessmen would make enormous profits selling it back in their own country. Making a profit was all that mattered. No consideration was given to the ocean that was taking more than its share of discards. No one paid any attention to all the raw materials that left the all-free nation—materials that could have been used to preserve or create new jobs in their own country.

Why didn't anyone see that if these raw materials were kept in their own country and made into products, it would have kept jobs for them? Was it because the business community had so much power it could do what it wanted at the expense of jobs in the all-free nation? Did the all-free demand such high wages and benefits that it was unprofitable for business? Was it greed on the part of the business community to make the greatest profit they could, even at the expense of their own country? What would the businessmen do when the all-free nation became a service nation, unable to manufacture items for its own needs?

Did government participate in this practice unwittingly?...By lack of concern?...A passive attitude?... Import rules which were too lax?...Too many controls on the business community?...So many questions—unanswered.

This plan went along well for some time until so many factories were located out of their own land that more and more workers were without jobs and therefore could no longer afford the items being sent in. *How could anyone control this practice? What would happen to their country when so many were without jobs? How many take-overs would occur with some companies becoming more and more powerful?* With this power came the financial ability to close any "unprofitable" plant and relocate anywhere they chose. Never mind the workers who had lost their jobs, they'd find work somewhere—*or would they? How much power would the rich need to completely control the poor?*

It only stands to reason that if the rich were "taking care of the poor" they would have a great deal to say in the way the poor lived.

When the people were taking care of their little pieces of land, they were using the land in the best possible manner. Everything was used and returned to the soil. Nature was at peace with itself. Even the little earth plowmen (earthworms) lived in the soil. But nature soon gave way to technology.

The plowmen who lived in the soil were poisoned, the birds left, there was nothing to eat, and the trees were gone. Everything was taken from the land and nothing returned to it.

Areas were drained to make way for larger areas. Water was sent along the path of least resistance until it ended up in the largest reservoir it could find. Government was paying to drain land and to grow crops on these lands. So many lands were drained it began to affect the natural cycle of nature. No individual could predict what effect his action would have but when all land owners began the same practices, there were consequences.

Companies became even larger. When they were small, people could communicate with people. Later, people communicated with machines. Everything became impersonal. All things had numbers. Not simple numbers that were easy to remember but large numbers that were on a card. If you did not know your number you could not use your card. Older people were completely left out—life was too complex. Buttons were pushed for everything. All information had to be put in a machine. No one needed to talk to anyone. It was as if it were no longer an accepted way to communicate.

Cards were used for all business transactions. You could use your card instead of money. Anyone could use their card to loan themselves money that they didn't have. Businesses became larger and larger.

There had been small shopkeepers who kept track of their stock and salespeople to help the customer with his selections. This became unprofitable. The stores had to enlarge to hold more and more items. It became an ordinary practice to have mostly shelf-stockers. Very few people were left to wait on the customers. They were only there to take your card. Of course with little supervision and all these shelves full, it was easy to see how shoplifting developed. Big business just wrote this into their budget instead of hiring more help. Shelves were stocked with items from other countries. No one paid any attention. No one even considered the fact that because workers in other countries earned less, the items should cost less. Big business just kept making profits at the expense of the people. And government didn't tax the profits reinvested in other countries, or collect an import tax on items made outside the all-free nation.

Meanwhile the country's debt was increasing at an alarming rate. With big business moving to countries where they could make the most profit, a new order was certainly coming to the world. Loyalty was exchanged for the profit of big business and their shareholders, yet if these factories were to be nationalized the money to reimburse the big businessman would come from the already burdened all-free taxpayers. Big business couldn't lose.

As these stores enlarged, the little stores could not compete. They fell by the wayside. No one paid any attention. After all, the public had to buy at the "best price they could". Larger companies bought each other. Expansion was the word.

How large did each company have to become to control the price of any item? How soon would it be before a company, not the consumer, decided what should be sold?

A person had a choice in the food they purchased. They would pick a brand they trusted, decide on the price, and if it was fair, they bought it. But the stores decided to have their own brands so they could increase their profits. It wasn't long before generic food took over, because the public could afford it. No one knew who was packaging their food anymore. No one took responsibility for quality. Then a curious event happened. Food prices began to climb. The very few large stores sold all the items at a price they agreed upon. No one had a choice anymore. (The underclass especially did not have a choice.) There were stores where the rich could still purchase anything they wanted but the others had to stand in line to buy their generic products.

So few in charge of so much. *Where would it end? Did big have to become bigger until it was all-encompassing?*

There was so much waste. It didn't become a problem right away. Packaging was the main reason. Everything came in a disposable wrap. Just buy the item and discard its surrounding. It would end up in the garbage, in someone's landfill far away where it wouldn't be seen again.

This was the way it was for a long time until finally so many items were sold in so much packaging that the ground couldn't hold everything. It rebelled and the ground water became contaminated. No one had cared what went into these landfills. *Surely the earth would purify it. But even nature had its limits. Why did people have to live as if they were the only ones? Why did companies make products with no regard to the waste created? Should there have been no consideration to the end result as long as the immediate needs were met? Was it wise to use as much as one could, never giving any regard to who else might be affected?*

Finally some began recycling. This was a slow process. People had to be convinced their life would be affected if they didn't participate. The rich, who used the most, were the last to participate. It was too much work. *Who wanted to separate everything into its own category? Why should they have to do it?* It was too easy to be wasteful. They could pay what ever the cost to get rid of their waste.

Did anyone care about the land anymore? What about all the timber that had been taken? Was it used to create jobs in the all-free land or sent to ocean ships to be cut and returned at a high price? If it was not used by the all-free people, should it have been saved for future use? What about the animals and birds that called the forest home; were they of no concern?

Was there a balance that could be met to keep nature on an even course?

Would jobs in recycling be created in lieu of this continuous timber cutting? Could the all-free people come to an agreement on land use before too many jobs had gone by the wayside, ground water polluted, forests destroyed, and business sent to other countries? Would the country ever return to quality standards instead of quantity standards? Clearly, the environment needed their help.

If paper waste constituted the largest contributor to landfills, would recycling turn the tide in controlling the amount added to landfills and at the same time save forests? Could people still have jobs cutting trees if exporting of the raw product was halted? Should a valuable natural resource have been sent outside the country when it took so many years to renew itself?

The factories also were not acting responsibly. Making a profit was the bottom line. Products and by-products were produced more rapidly year after year. No one cared if the ground water was fouled or the air polluted. Man was going to make a good life for himself no matter what the consequences.

Consequences were not even thought of. Of course the rule was—if it didn't affect you—it wasn't happening.

Surely a little dirty smoke wouldn't hurt—it never did before.

No one even thought of testing the ground water or even questioning the purity of the water factories discharged every day. No one could question big business anyway. There was too much bureaucracy to even find who might be responsible and be able to change the practices taking place.

It would have been so easy to correct these matters if anyone had taken the time. Of course it would have cost money and profit had to be the bottom line. *But what would the final cost be when all the profit takers left the area? Would the residue be around to weaken future generations? Was it even going to matter? What about the present? Should they have been thinking of their children and themselves? Why couldn't products have been made with a thought beforehand of how to disarm the chemicals produced and make them into unharmful products?*

If the all-free people were so intelligent as to make all these things, then it could have been assumed they could have made harmless by-products too. But the cost would have been more. More now, but less later. *Did anyone care about later?*

They even made buildings to supply their areas with light, not even giving a thought to the by-product of by-products. This by-product was even dangerous.

The operation of the building was even dangerous, producing contaminated water that would be around for centuries in exchange for the short benefit they were deriving. The waste residue had to be buried in thick concrete or in mountains or sent into space. *Why couldn't these people think beforehand of what effect their action may have had on their country? Did anyone think? Did any profit maker ever consider quality standards instead of quantity standards? How much "stuff" did the all-free people or any people need?*

WHAT WAS THE "GOOD LIFE?"

Maybe there was a line that needed to be drawn to protect land use and jobs with consideration given to the country as a whole, instead of business looking only at financial gain—*or would man attempt to control nature to such an extent that he would end his own existence and only nature would prevail?*

CHAPTER III - EDUCATION

The schools in the free nation were community schools. Children went to school within a few miles of where they lived. Many grades were taught by one teacher. This changed. Schools were built in towns. Each town had at least one school or more, as needed. Parents were involved in school activities and children who went to school together played together after school. They even had neighborhood parks where children were safe. It was the best of times for children.

Now times were changing. Schools were being consolidated and becoming larger. This was happening over the whole land. It was felt that schools could offer more classes with a wide range of subjects, many sports activities and cultural events. *This was fine up to a point but how large was too large? At what point did a community lose control over its school? When a school became too large with a large amount of money coming from the government did government have the right to mandate the subject matter? Who was government?*

When children went to school, they were safe. Discipline and order were kept in the classroom. The principal had authority and children knew they would visit him if they didn't behave. Then new-found freedom developed. They needed open study halls with classmates as monitors. Of course, peers were unable to maintain discipline with peers. Therefore, study halls became unruly. This also led to the right to choose classes the student selected. They even had open hours when they didn't have to attend classes. This led to lack of order. If a child was to attend school, the object was to learn something, but the all-free people felt freedom to choose and freedom to do what they wanted outweighed structured classes.

If children did not have discipline and structure, they were then free to act and do what they wanted. *Did the free people want freedom without responsibility?* They had so many government restrictions that everyone in authority was unable to demand responsibility of children. If a child would do what they asked, it was fine. If the child didn't want to do something, he had the right not to do it, too. Lawyers would get involved in this argument. The Liberty Union of the all-free people would get involved. *Why couldn't the rights that do the most good be put into effect? Didn't the unruly affect the children who would follow rules?*

It seemed this lack of order finally affected the schools and lack of discipline became an even greater problem.

Children began carrying weapons to school. Even law officers had to patrol hallways to protect children from each other and protect teachers from some children. Instead of schools being a fun and safe place, they were becoming uncontrollable.

Did this happen because they were too large and impersonal? Was too little expected of the children? Were freedoms given to the few at the expense of the majority? Why didn't the all-free people make their schools safe? Parents who cared about their children wanted them to have a childhood free of worries. *Why didn't parents band together and demand safety for their children? Were they too busy in their own lives? Did they feel that they would be a target of someone if they tried to demand more of their schools? Why couldn't unruly children have been kept together in one classroom away from the main body of students, even in a separate building until they learned what was expected of them? Why did the few have rights that superseded the rights of the majority? How could anyone justify a society where rights for the most good were ignored?*

Some felt that school dress codes would deter crime. If children wore the same clothing, competition would be lessened. This was true, but the basic problem went deeper than this. Surely the way a child dresses and what his parents could afford determined, many times, what group the child would fit into. Having the same clothing could prevent stealing in school but the basic problem wasn't solved.

Surely there would always be some with money and some without as much. *Shouldn't the basic problem of lack of responsibility and lack of moral training have been addressed? Why didn't the all-free people address the basic problems? Was it easier to follow the path of least resistance?*

Even the morals of the children were being affected by government rules. The government knew what was best for the children—even better than the parents did. Instead of responsible behavior being taught to correct the problem of the great Affliction, "protection" was passed out freely to the children without parental permission. Young children saw this as easy "protection" that would keep them "free" of disease. Now there was no reason to follow moral behavior, they were "safe." The parents didn't have any say in this matter—the government was going to "protect" their children even if the parents felt this wasn't the best way to handle the problem. "Protection" was used instead of *abstinence*. Many parents were upset because their authority was undermined. The parents' voice didn't matter and the schools were not in the business of teaching morals. *The government knew best.*

Drugs were also a problem. They were everywhere. Uncontrolled. No one seemed to know how to stop the drug invasion. Money was to be made. Everyone wanted to "get high" to feel their best—to get in touch with their inner selves.

Children bought drugs like candy—it was easy to find someone who sold them. Many parents did not realize their children were using drugs. They didn't even take the time to notice. Needles were even used to take some drugs—they were even shared and this added to the great Affliction. The all-free government tried to curb this use by education. Some even passed out clean needles and the drug use continued. *Why were solutions so complicated? Was there too much money involved? Did groups who benefited from this money have a say in the laws that were passed?*

Other drugs were controlled by the government by registration—*was this so much different?* Very little money was given to help addicts overcome drug use. There were groups who helped each other overcome addictions of many kinds. *Why didn't the all-free government begin with the help of these groups? Why didn't the government set up centers with medical personnel overseeing the drug distribution? If the people insisted on buying the drugs, why couldn't medical personnel administer these intercepted drugs at a price that would undercut the dealers and offer help to these users at the same time?* Instead of controlling these drugs they talked about legalizing them.

It was as if government couldn't participate in a solution. No matter how many shipments of drugs were intercepted, many more got through.

Some talked of penalties for drug dealers. *"Why weren't the penalties swift and sure?"* they wondered. The drugs were disrupting society. *Why were solutions so slow in coming? Were there any solutions or was society headed on a downward course?*

Children needed to be safe and have places for activity. *Did the all-free society forget about the children? Would they even need to take drugs if they had other things to do? Surely the money they could earn from selling drugs was better than they could earn elsewhere. But what about the children who were spending their money? Didn't they realize that this money could have had a better use? Or did they feel if they had extra money someone would steal it from them? Was there so much pressure to fit in with their group that the ability to say "no" was lost?*

Would smaller community schools have been an answer to these problems? Surely people had more control when they knew each other. Maybe sending children many miles away from home by bus contributed to isolation and fear on the part of the children. *Why couldn't good use be made of neighborhoods?* Even with high buildings to live in there should have been a way to make it safe for children to play. There had to be areas where families could go to do things together.

Neighborhood parks had once been common.

Not many years later, people lived in fear of sending their children to these parks. Even *they* would not go to the park. *Why did this change occur? Why was safety such a problem? Didn't anyone care about anyone else? What kind of society could exist when only the criminal element had control?* The all-free society was finding out the answers to all these questions. Meanwhile, the poorest people, who were affected the most—didn't venture out after dark. Many didn't want to go out during the day alone, either. They lived in fear, yet very few did anything about it.

In the all-free land, there also were many other serious problems that affected both children and adults. One of these was the problem people faced because of the color of their skin. It was hard for some to overcome their prejudices because they were one color and another person was another color. These prejudices were passed on to their children. All people were equal, yet many thought the color of their skin made them superior. Many didn't give the other person a chance to show his capabilities. This caused a split in the country by causing social isolation. Laws were passed to help minorities, but no law could be strong enough if people did not feel in their hearts that everyone was equal.

Education made people aware of problems but, by itself, could not change attitudes unless moral ideals were included in the teachings.

CHAPTER IV - HEALTH

There were many arguments among the people. These arguments came about because the health care of their nation was in peril. Cost for care had grown beyond their reach. It had always been expensive to get sick; now it was beyond the ability of most to pay for care.

The all-free people considered health care a business instead of a public service and, as a result, costs escalated. In business, profit was made because a product was produced. There was virtually no limit on profit when a product could be sold, purchased by an ever-increasing number of people who desired the product. In health care the limit on profit was determined by the ability of the consumer to pay for the service. When the ability of the consumers to pay had reached its limit, there was no further profit. Therefore, the difference had to be made up or the profit controlled. *If the all-free nation was to remain free, it could not control profit. What could it do?*

Knowledge and skill had escalated in the latter years. The medical community could treat disease with an ever increasing array of technology. To supply these treatments was costly. There were also more and more elderly people who had worked hard all their lives to save for retirement years. Many times these years were undermined by illness that was becoming increasingly expensive. Other people went without medical care because they couldn't afford to carry "coverage insurance". They needed all the money they could earn, simply to live. Even the most minor cost was out of reach for them, so they neglected medical care.

A system was developed to pool the money of workers to insure these people against illness cost. At first, this worked well. If a person visited a doctor or hospital, some of the cost would be paid from the pool of money the insurance company had collected. Insurance companies became profitable from this money and grew large and powerful. The companies invested this money in buildings and projects. Some of the money was used to pay the bills of the people they insured. The companies wanted to keep as much of this money as they could to continue with their growth, so they devised a plan to control the cost of illness. They determined how much an illness should cost and how many days a person would be allowed to remain in the hospital for a particular illness. This would have been a good idea if someone would have monitored the use of the profits of the insurance company itself.

What percent of their income was used to actually pay the cost of the insured and how much was used for their own growth? Were the health insurance companies money managers for all the people who pooled their money to pay for medical costs they incurred, or were they mainly interested in profit for their company?

In years past each community had a hospital. With the expansion of technology, these small hospitals could not keep up with the larger hospitals. Many small hospitals closed or else went into debt trying to keep up. *Why didn't the small hospitals treat the illnesses that they could handle and send the patients who needed more extensive care to the larger hospitals?* These patients could have returned home to recuperate in their own community. The cost would have been less because only the hospitals in the large cities would have needed so much equipment. Other uses could have been sought to keep these small hospitals operating. For instance, there were many drug addicts with no treatment facilities available.

About the same time the explosion of technology took place, patients began suing their doctor if a less-than-desirable outcome resulted from his care. The doctor, to protect himself and also his patients, purchased malpractice insurance. This worked out well at first, but as jury awards for injury became greater, the cost for this insurance climbed. This cost added to everyone's medical bill.

Would this cost have been so great if limits had been placed on the award given to the injured? Why wasn't a logical limit set to protect the cost for everyone? Even juries felt the insurance companies with their endless supply of money could pay huge settlements to the person who won a malpractice suit. Hardly anyone questioned that the lawyer got a percentage of the award and not a set fee for his work. This made many lawyers rich. The cost for medical care became a burden for all of society. Doctors fees, hospital charges and costs of medicine all escalated. This was caused because there was no way to control profit. If extra money was made, it was spent on new facilities and equipment even if it really wasn't needed. The hospitals and doctors could get more money with this expansion. Only the small hospitals were affected because of expansion. The doctor could move to a larger community. Guaranteed coverage from government and insurance plans made up the difference between what a person could actually pay and the cost of service or medicine. This fact enabled the charge to go beyond a realistic cost.

There were many new diseases that came to the all-free people. In the old days, people had been quarantined before they entered the country to be sure no new disease was introduced. In the latter days there was world travel and no one even thought of quarantining people anymore.

A quarantine would have been against the principles of the all-free people. As a result, they assimilated these diseases—even the great Affliction.

It was also against the principles of their freedom to test for this Affliction; therefore it was kept a secret. No one knew who had this disease; therefore, everyone needed to protect themselves from everyone else. In the past, when a disease had no cure—the people with the disease were isolated from the rest of society until a cure could be found. But the freedom of the individual was now uppermost; therefore society had to cope with the Affliction in the best manner that was available. They used "protection" for sex, did not share needles, and the flowing life source was screened for the Affliction. For the most part this worked well, but the only problem was, no one knew when or if the Affliction was in their body until they were sick. It sometimes took years for this sickness to come forth. It seemed a foolish risk to scatter this disease in society where no one knew it existed, but this was how it was done. Even medical personnel did not know if the person they cared for was infected. They were told to use comprehensive provisions to contain all bodily fluids.

Until a cure was found, this disease was not contained anywhere in the whole world, and it was not known how many people were infected because not everyone had been tested.

How many people would need to die before the whole of society's right to know had precedence over the individual's right? Laws were passed to force medical personnel to treat and care for people with the Affliction, even if the caregiver did not want to put himself or his family at risk. *Certainly these people needed care; but could a way have been found to treat these people by using personnel who already had the Affliction in their body?*

It would have been easier for the all-free people to protect themselves from what they knew rather than from what they didn't know. *When the people with the Affliction became too ill to care for themselves, would it have been better for society as a whole to care for these people in specific units where all caregivers would have been aware of what they were dealing with? Didn't it make sense to keep exposure to all caregivers at a minimum rather than to place these people randomly in care facilities where they were not identified?* Surely the risk of a healthy person to a disease that had no cure should have had consideration. To use comprehensive containment measures had merit, but it could have been argued that even extra care could be used when a person was aware of a specific disease. In emergency situations, rapid action was/is needed, and this action, because of its nature, could have led to accidental exposure to the caregiver. At least, if a caregiver knew the diagnosis, his own protection would have been uppermost in case of a deadly illness. If he did not know, he may have reacted to the situation before thinking of himself.

The rights of the caregiver were even taken away. The caregivers were forced to take care of people with this deadly illness, even if these caregivers felt the security of their own families was at stake. With this disease not becoming evident in a person's body for years, and also with no cure for this illness, it seemed a very unfair decision.

The protection of a healthy person should have had precedence over an illness that had no cure.

To try to contain this Affliction, some people talked about testing immigrants before they entered the all-free nation, as they once had. Many people argued that this mandatory act prevented the immigrant people from the freedom to decide if they wanted to be tested. *Was this right given to people even before they were a citizen of the all-free land? Should these people have been allowed to carry a disease with no cure into the all-free land?* Even school children in the all-free land had to be protected by immunization against other diseases before they could attend school. No one said these children could attend school without following these requirements.

It seemed that diseases which had a treatment were contained by requiring immunization, but this disease that had no cure was allowed to be assimilated into society.

Should any disease that had no cure be allowed to run rampant in society until a cure was found?

CHAPTER V - CRIME

The laws had been followed. People knew that they were necessary for the good of the majority. But the laws finally became so overwhelming that order was destroyed. Even the criminals, whose rights had been taken away when they entered prison, were given rights. They were treated so well that there was no punishment. It was as if people felt sorry for them because they had committed a crime. Even the death penalty was nearly abolished. People said it didn't deter crime. Some argued that at least the criminal who was put to death would never do any damage again. Instead, lawyers could put in appeal after appeal for the one they represented. It seemed no one cared about the one who was hurt as long as the law was followed to protect the rights of the criminal.

The free people had a communication system that could give access to anyone who wanted to watch a trial. The accused person's face was shown but the accuser's face was obliterated. In the system of not guilty until guilt was proven, it seemed ironic that it was the one who was proving his innocence whose identity was known. *Should either have been identified until guilt was proven?*

Many criminals wanted to prove they were insane so they could be treated instead of sent to prison. Some couldn't understand why, if a person was insane, he still shouldn't serve the same amount of time as a person who was not insane. They thought that if the crime was committed, the punishment should have been equal. Victims lived in fear that someone would be released before they were rehabilitated. How could anyone know for sure what was in another's mind? At least equal penalties would keep someone out of society for a predetermined amount of time. Plea bargaining was a tool also used to get a lighter sentence. Victims also lived in fear that someone would be paroled too soon.

A system of protection was set up for the criminal. Once they were proven guilty, they were confined. But this was not the end. No permanent guidelines were set. Even if a person was guilty beyond any reasonable doubt he could still appeal his sentence. Any new information could be introduced, any technicality brought up, and because of these rules, criminals were released even when everyone knew specifically it was they who committed the crimes. It became ridiculous. There were too many contradictory rules.

Not only was this a problem, but not enough facilities were available to hold the law breakers. This meant that many were out in society who had no right to be there. This sent the wrong message to these people.

Without any real punishment, many felt it must have been all right with society to act as they did. *After all, they were not to blame—it was the lessons that were not taught while they were young.* People said prison was like a revolving door. What was good for the criminals was bad for society. So much money was spent for trials to find out if a person was guilty. This money was spent in vain when prison sentences could not be carried out for the time designated because of overcrowding. People stopped reporting crime. *"What good did it do?"* they asked. They would only be dragged through court year after year to relive an event they wanted to forget.

Drug abuse was one reason there was so much crime. Drugs were expensive. Stealing to get money was common. Some wondered, *"Why were people buying drugs? Was their use an escape from reality?" If peoples' living situations improved—would they need drugs? If drugs were affecting the whole of society to such an extent, why was the situation often ignored? Could people be responsible on their job if they had been taking drugs? Why couldn't strict laws have been passed to guarantee swift and sure penalties for those selling drugs?*

It was very disruptive to a society to have people using substances that altered their minds to the extent the drugs did. *Why wasn't money spent to set up centers to help? Wasn't society worth the expense of changing this situation?*

The person who took the drugs and spent his money for them needed help desperately. When people were satisfied with their lives they used their money for other things that would have made them happy. *Was life so unliveable for these people that drugs were the only way? Other drugs were controlled by the government—why couldn't illegal drugs be controlled? Was the good life feeling "high"? Were these users bent on self-destruction? Could a free society continue, when a large segment of it needed drugs to exist? Laws had been passed to protect people from using other substances—why was this so much different?*

There was so much money connected to this drug use. The all-free people had to figure out why people were buying the drugs in the first place. If there were no buyers, there would be no sellers. Anything people could make money on they would do.

Some wondered whether the few who wanted to disrupt society should have been allowed to do it by intimidating others. There had always been people who had lived on the edges of society. *Why were they invading the mainstream? Was the main body of society deteriorating to such an extent that it felt this was the way to live? Did people lack self discipline so they were unable to determine right from wrong? Did they care so little for each other that no one felt responsibility to protect the vulnerable? Were neighborhoods going to be made safe again so people would be free to come and go?*

Could the drug problem be shrunk to the edge of society so as not to affect the whole body? There were so many questions and no answers were forthcoming.

Maybe there was no edge to society anymore. *With all the freedoms that everyone had, who knew right from wrong?* Churches were still teaching the old ways but slowly even their teachings were questioned. People felt that the old laws could be changed to conform to this modern society.

Rules were there to keep order in a society. Surely it was not always possible to follow a rule, but there were consequences when it was not followed. Individual discipline came from conscious decisions that a person made in learning right from wrong. This also was taught in the home. If rules were not followed, there were consequences. Even in a home, each person was affected by another's actions.

But discipline was not even a word anymore. This came about because people had used discipline to inflict physical punishment. In later days, physical punishment was no longer accepted, which was as it should have been. But they forgot that discipline had a more important meaning. It meant following rules that should have been set, by training and instruction from their parents. Parents were not controlling their children's behavior.

This affected all of society because even teachers lost control in the classroom. They had to try to keep order instead of teaching subjects.

The all-free society could not determine why education for the children was not as productive as it had been in the old days. Schools had become larger and more impersonal. Individual help was out of the question. Many students were left by the wayside and some of these students became disruptive.

It was difficult to teach and to learn. Parents were too busy or couldn't help with homework and many students didn't care if it was even done. Administration was cumbersome and distant because it had grown too large. Some wondered if smaller would have been better, but everything was geared for growth.

Even criminals were taught college courses. Some argued against this. *"Was it fair to get a college degree in prison?"* some questioned. It would have been more logical to teach a job skill to these people, and when they were released, they could pay for college themselves. It seemed so many benefits were given to criminals and no one was able to question the wisdom of these decisions. The all-free society continued to give more and more privileges because all rights were questioned by the criminals. *Should a criminal have any rights beyond a comfortable environment?* Some criminals were even demanding they should profit from their crime. Books were written with enormous profits. The victim was left behind and forgotten.

Was the criminal justice system inept? Did the criminals figure this out before anyone else? It seemed like the lawyers were on "their side." Who was paying these lawyers? Was most of the money coming from society's funds?

The courts' hands were tied. Law upon law was passed to protect the criminals. When the criminal's case was brought to trial, if it got that far, evidence was thrown out because it wasn't obtained in a correct manner. More and more criminals went free on a technicality.

Justice was not served. There were too many instructions to juries. When people went free because of a technicality, it seemed as if common sense had no place in the justice system. Some felt that if someone committed a crime and it was absolutely known that that person were guilty, no matter what technicality occurred, the person who committed the crime should have had to pay for it. If justice was not served the system would fall apart.

CHAPTER VI - WAR

A war happened in those days too. It was a short war, to the amazement of everyone who participated in it. Never before had the country been so united, even though not everyone believed there was a reason to fight.

What really happened was that the men and women who were called to serve were mostly from the mainstream of society. They had been week-end warriors. This made a great difference. Now everyone was connected to the war in some way by knowing personally someone who was going to give of themselves so another people could remain all-free. It was an evil time for some. Rulers were ready to take charge and dictate their own agendas to gain power.

One particular leader saw his chance to begin advancement to overtake a people with no defense. It was in this leader's best interest to become even more powerful to gain for himself all the riches. After all, no one would stop him.

He was an absolute dictator. Even the all-free people told him they would not stop him. They were afraid to antagonize his friends in case they were on *his* side.

The all-powerful's army advanced into this little country taking advantage of the people. They took over all the functions in this tiny country disrupting the lives of all its citizens. No one in recent times could remember how destructive an army could be, especially if their leader was driven by greed. But they soon found out. Now all the friends who ruled the neighboring areas became alarmed that this absolute leader may decide that their country was next on his agenda. *What did it matter what he did before this, if it did not affect them? Would the all-free people help before this army advanced taking more and more?*

The all-free people found it in their best interest to control this absolute leader. Not only to stop his advancement but to send his army home. If this all-powerful leader were allowed to continue, he would have so much wealth, it wouldn't be long and he would control a large part of the world and its resources, and possibly disrupt the lives of the all-free people. A war was a small disruption—the alternative would be a major disruption, possibly even changing the all-free nation to be controlled by the all-powerful nation sometime in the distant future.

The all-free people quickly sent their armies and best equipment. This was done to prevent any advancement this leader may have had in mind.

When the all-free people heard stories of what had taken place in the invaded little country, they realized this absolute leader's armies must not remain. A civilized people could not condone what the all-powerful's armies had done to the small nation. This meant that a war was inevitable. *"But how were they to get his armies out?"* they asked. It would have to be a rapid advancement that was immediate and forceful.

The all-powerful nation had a weapon that many in the all-free nation had never even thought he would use. But, the all-powerful leader decided to use it. Possibly with its use, he could convince others to be on his side.

He lobbed his missiles at unprotected people, trying to antagonize them to retaliate, but the all-free people insisted upon restraint. They wanted to be sure that when this war started, they would know whom they could count on to be on their side. It was a very difficult spot to be in.

While all of this was taking place, the all-free nation had direct communication from within this all-powerful nation. In fact, before the war, some all-free people had set up a broadcasting facility in the capital of the all-powerful nation. This news was being broadcast periodically for everyone to listen to.

This was fine before the war started, and after the war started, almost everyone in the all-free nation felt that this was an important source of information. *Why should anyone care that the information was censored? They knew what buildings were hit, didn't they? They even knew that civilian targets were hit. Especially when civilians were injured. (Never mind the destruction the all-powerful leader did to the people in the little country. That could be forgotten. Was it only the casualties the all-free people caused that should be added up?)*

Both sides were poised for an all out war. Just how it would begin no one knew except the leaders, of course. Everyone had their own ideas, even thinking the all-powerful leader would back out of the little country and return the situation to the *status quo.* That was not to be. He was going to win the spoils of war.

The time was set to stop the invasion of the all-powerful's army into the little country. No one was prepared for how quickly the troops would move or how many planes would fly over enemy territory. It was a blur; the all-free and the allied nations meshed like clockwork. For the most part, even the missiles that were lobbed to civilian targets by the all-powerful were stopped in mid-air (although a few got through which brought much sadness). It was impossible to know what the outcome of the war would have been if the all-free people had no defense against them.

Surely many felt that risking so many lives to save such a small country from the all-powerful was not worth it. The all-powerful leader knew this to be true, but he miscalculated. As it turned out, the enemy, because they were *controlled* by their leader, could not retreat or surrender. The all-free did not want to annihilate them, but had no choice. Many targets were hit in the all-powerful's country. The all-free leader was trying to find the command post of the all-powerful. *They destroyed some of his communications, but where was he?*

At the same time, all the people in the world were getting information on the war, and what was happening, from the all-free communication center in the land of the all-powerful. No one in the all-free nation dared to disrupt this communication. Planes must avoid it. The word must continue. The all-powerful leader knew this. The main reason the all-powerful leader had allowed this communication center in his country was to protect himself. He knew no one from the all-free nation would destroy their own communications. He was very crafty. (Everyone would have been in an uproar about not being directly informed how the war was going.) They were so spoiled. *How could a war be conducted when civilians were allowed to remain in this manner, especially when a war was in progress?*

Advancing through the little country, no one could believe the destruction the all-powerful's army had caused.

Not only this, but they had stolen everything of value while they were there. In their retreat they had set every oil well in the the tiny country on fire. Smoke was spewing everywhere. *Was this a selfish act to tell the world, "If I can't have this oil, no one else can"? Does any single person or group have the right to contaminate the earth in this manner? When the fires were out and the oil mess cleaned up, would every-one soon forget what was done?* The all-powerful leader was very cunning. When he felt the all-free would attack by sea he opened the oil wells and spilled as much oil as would run out of the wells into the sea. There was no end to this oil. It would contam-inate everything. It had to be filtered out of the water. No one knew to what extent the habitat of wildlife or sea creatures would be disrupted.

From now on the attack would have to continue to advance on the ground. The all-free army advanced almost to the area where the all-powerful leader had his best troops. But then a surprise occurred. The all-free leader called a halt to the war. To advance meant casualties because the war up to now had mainly been an air war, so very few lives had been risked.

The all-free leader knew if he caused many casualties on his side, no one would be happy with him. He may not even get reelected. Therefore, the leader of the all-powerful nation was saved. His bunker under the communication area of the all-free was preserved.

After that time of war, people even forgot the questions to ask. *Where was the all-powerful leader now? What was he up to? Was he capable of gathering as many weapons of destruction again? Was he still hiding his most dangerous weapons of destruction? As long as he had money, would people be willing to make a profit to accommodate him? Was the oil still causing problems on the land and in the water? Who paid for this devastation? Why did the all-powerful leader have any say in the affairs of his country?* He lost the war but still remained a threat to the world.

To make matters worse, the all-free leader had encouraged minority groups to rebel against the all-powerful leader. But when they did, the all-free leader felt it was not possible to come to their aid. Untold suffering was caused to these people. Economic sanctions continued against the all-powerful leader, and hopefully these sanctions would bring him down. In the meantime the sanctions caused much suffering to the all-powerful's innocent people.

The all-powerful leader was enjoying his success even if he didn't win the war. He was still an absolute dictator, continuing with his cunning plans. The world was safe for now—*or was it?*

CHAPTER VII - DESTRUCTION

There was chaos in the cities of the all-free people. It was reminiscent of the days when some all-powerful people were starting over. Long lines were everywhere. Even some of the wealthy had to stand in line, but mostly it was the underclass, whom the rich had been taking advantage of these past years. No one knew who was in charge. It was hard to know anything anymore. The past seemed so far away.

Times had been very good to the all-free people. They seemed to have everything. *What could bring about such a turn of events to such a good nation?* Everyone was asking the same question.

Was it an illusion? Had the times been that good?

The all-free people finally realized, too late, that government had become too large.

It began when the all-free people decided to give up a standard for their money.

This was a brilliant idea, on the part of the decision makers. As much money as was needed could be printed, within certain guidelines. Now more money was available to expand business. In their eyes, this was good for the country. There was phenomenal growth. About the same time the "card" was coming into being. Before the "card" very few items were purchased without the money to pay for them. After the card, all a person had to have was enough money to meet a payment. This was a boon to business. A great amount of products could be sold and the store would even get extra money from the lenders. It was such a good idea.

This was wonderful for as long as it lasted. But there was an end. It began with greed and lack of responsibility. Anyone could get a card and limits were out of control. Businesses knew there were enough responsible people to cover the loss of the ones who took on too much debt and were unable to pay. What they didn't count on was that generations were changing. The old way was unknown by many. The card was known now. Everything went along smoothly until jobs were lost. With job loss went the ability to keep up payments. Very few had savings to tide them over. Now everyone was on the brink of a catastrophe.

Building had been phenomenal. No one had seen such growth. But was it all good? Most thought so. Money and investment was the wave of the future.

But where were the farms? What was happening to the land and water? Were any trees missing? No one noticed.

The cities became larger and larger. Everything became more impersonal. Little stores and communities were destroyed to make way for progress. The rich moved away from the cities to give their families the good life. They only worked in the cities to get money. The poor lived in the cities (in the impersonal existence) never knowing when their building was next on the destruction agenda. Crime began to escalate.

The all-free nation had needed guns in the past. They were hunters, and guns were necessary to obtain food and for their protection.

In later days, it was decided that shells for guns should be registered. This was done to keep track of those who owned guns. After all, guns were not necessary for hunting anymore. Food could be obtained in stores, and hunting was mostly for sport. Criminals were beginning to use guns at an unprecedented rate. Now guns needed to be registered. The law abiding citizens gave up their guns. (The criminal kept his). Guns were dangerous and needed to be secured. *This was true, but was it the best decision? Were the law abiding citizens putting themselves at risk? Would the criminal use his gun less if he controlled matters?*

Law abiding citizens wouldn't have a need to use a gun if they were not in jeopardy. *Surely guns were out of control but shouldn't laws have been passed to make swift and sure penalties to illegal gun users instead of taking guns away from the "good" people?*

The situation got out of hand. The all-free people in favor of a gun free society had their way. No one had a gun anymore, that is, of ordinary people. The military had guns, the police had guns and the criminals had guns. *Did this make people more safe?*

The government became more and more centralized to improve services for the people. Decisions that affected more and more people came from farther and farther away. Laws were made to protect people, yet no one stated they wanted protection. These laws that were passed took away the rights of the individual to make decisions for themselves. The government said these laws were passed to protect the citizens from their own actions.

Centralized leadership assumed more responsibility in taking care of people. Basic living expenses were provided for an ever increasing population. *How many services could be provided before the system would become overloaded? How impersonal would a system become when large numbers of people needed help?*

Was there any accountability on the part of citizens who received these services? It became like a self-perpetuating machine. *Was there anyway to get out of the system once you were in? Did anyone want to get out of such a helpful system?*

The people paid taxes to help run their government. The people with the most money paid the least. They were able to avoid being taxed because they could hide their income in business expenses and programs that were designed for them. The government felt this idea kept the economy going. *But where was the actual money coming from that was spent to keep government going?* Mainly from the people between the rich and the poor. It was easy to see what they owed in taxes. Records were methodically kept by employers who reported to government. There was no way to hide income, as the wealthy did. Besides, someone had to pay the expenses of government.

The rich kept making more and more money. The ones between rich and poor needed their money to live and the poor had to be taken care of. When the rich kept their money they invested it in business but most of their business was now invested outside of the free nation where they lived. They made more profit this way.

Many jobs were lost in their own all-free country because almost everything they bought was made elsewhere.

People were standing in line to collect money for not working. Their ability to buy had dwindled.

The raw materials had left the country, boxcars and shiploads full of raw materials—year after year. Iron was gone along with the trees. Now the all-free nation had given all that it could give. Most factories had closed. They couldn't even make weapons for their own protection.

The only positive thing that was left were the farms. But they were large farms and had become larger. In some ways they were ineffective. They produced only a selected few crops. If these crops failed all profit was lost. They were told what to plant. Most decisions were made at a higher level.

The all-free nation was overwhelmed with plastic and paper. Some of these materials had been recycled but mountains more were in landfills. The water had become contaminated. New ways were used to purify water but they were slow and tedious. All this waste could have been prevented but the good life had been too important. Ways could have been found to keep the surroundings clean but mostly no one cared. The land which supported them so well was used so it had no more to give. The animals, which once were abundant, were down to a fraction of what they were. Many felt animals were not important; it was they, the people, who mattered. What they did not realize was that what was happening to the animals was only an indication of soon what was to follow—for them.

If only they would have used and not misused. If only the water were pure again and trees planted to replace the ones they used. If only there had been management with the good of the country (and the world) in mind. Instead, there had been greed and unconcern.

Pollution was already in the ground water. *What was happening to the lakes and rivers?* For years, they had become filled with agricultural runoff, even the land itself went into the lakes and rivers by the use of dams. Sewage from homes and salt from highways even went into the lakes. Now these lakes were also becoming congested with weeds that spread like wildfire. Of course because they were a free people— no one could interfere with anyone else's use of a lake. Instead of quarantining a lake and insisting on only one lake use—everyone was allowed to go from lake to lake. (People were supposed to check for weeds before they entered another lake). Not everyone was responsible; therefore, the weeds became out of control.

Did people's individual freedoms have precedence even when it was proven how devastating such action could be? What about the cost, and eventually when the majority of lakes were filled with weeds— would they have to be quarantined to save the few that were left?

Farms were very large and used to grow crops. Animals didn't live on farms anymore.

These animals were penned up to be constantly fed until they were large enough to use. Even hens were kept in small cages and were programmed to lay their eggs. Everything was set up for efficiency. Disease was more predominant because of this confinement. Of course government with *quantity* standards instead of quality standards didn't worry much about the animals and poultry. Instead of taking care of the hens to make sure they were healthy and would have uncontaminated eggs, a law was passed to cook eggs longer. No one even thought to ask why the eggs could no longer be eaten the old way.

The railroads, which were an economical way to transport freight, gave way to trucks. Decision makers never even considered having more trains from point to point with trucks going the shorter distances. More gas was used and the tax on the gas was used to pay for highways. *Why were the railways forgotten?*

Government was taking care of more and more. Not many people were economically aware, nor did they seem to care; nobody had to deny themselves anything.

Many all-free people were talking about spending less on the military. They felt this was an unnecessary expense because some all-powerful nations were broken up and were no longer a threat. Some talked about maintaining the strength of the military—this was called a waste of money by others.

After all-who wanted to waste money on protec-
tion when all-powerful nations were dissolving?

Should protection have been a priority? How
much protection? Was there always a person some-
where gaining enough power to try to overwhelm
another? Could a country be safe if it wasn't as strong
as its strongest potential adversary? Week-end war-
riors were used once—would they be needed again?

Hopefully sound judgments were used when
calculating their military spending cuts. A certain
amount of faith was necessary when considering
another nation's promises, or ability to wage war.

Everyone wanted peace. *True, everyone want-*
ed peace; but at what price and what cost? Should
the all-free nation risk being unprepared? Would they
miscalculate the designs and wants of other aspiring
nations? Would they have time to prepare and re-arm
again? Would the all-free people be the next victims
of some potential dictator? (The all-powerful leader
wanted peace if he could be in charge.) At least there
was peace now, and the weapons themselves were
under attack. *If the weapons were all destroyed how*
many people would be left who could make more?

CHAPTER VIII - GREED

The land of the all-free was becoming corrupt, destroying itself from the inside. Greed was rampant. Money was uppermost in most peoples' minds. *How could they get more money?* This was on everyone's agenda. Money—money—money. If anyone had enough money, they still needed more. No one had a definition of what enough money would be. It was always more than what they had. Money itself was not the problem. It was the corruption of people because of this relentless search for wealth.

Even nature itself was destroyed for money. Animals and sea life were killed for financial gain. Chemicals were put on the land to enrich it but at the same time destroyed it. Chemicals polluted water everywhere. Trees and plants were cut to make way for more buildings. Life seemed to be moving more rapidly. Civilization was almost running. Only a few short years ago, the country had been mostly open land. Now buildings and houses and people were everywhere.

Hardly any person all through history had ever lived in the spot of land where each of these houses were built. The serenity of beautiful snow covered lakes lined with trees was still in view but fading. The birds still sat in the branches, carefree, living each day with no thought to the future. *As their numbers dwindled could anyone say how many years were ahead? Would this society also vanish silently?*

Seeking the good life, people came from everywhere to the all-free land. This was not a problem until the numbers became overwhelming. In the free land, society tried to support these people. There was an enormous difference in the standard of living. Many immigrants had very little; therefore, it put a strain on the economic structure of the all-free nation. Disease was also a problem. The government was in a dilemma because of the freedoms they professed. They could not limit the immigrants or test for diseases. More and more people came. The country was losing the common thread that held their society together. People even challenged the language spoken by the all-free society. These "new" people wanted society to change for them. They wanted all that the good life offered, too. Besides, they would work for less because less was more than what they had.

The businessman was in control. After all, he was the one who did the employing. There wouldn't be jobs without him.

He was important. He should get the best wages for himself. The ones who worked for him were dispensable. After all, many needed jobs now. No one could argue that businesses needed profits to operate. The businessman argued that he should have low taxes so his business could continue to expand with with the use of these profits. Companies made profits and reinvested them in other countries' factories to make more profits. At the same time, the standard of living was shrinking for many people in the all-free nation. There was less work and more people.

The government in the all-free land couldn't keep up with all the maneuvers these business people used to avoid paying taxes. Big business could avoid paying taxes to help run the country but the small worker continued to pay "his fair share." After all, if it wasn't for big business, there would be no employers.

Government became like a machine. It didn't matter who was elected because the government structure was in place. This structure was difficult to interrupt and therefore any change was almost impossible. This happened because government became too centralized. As more bureaucracy was structured in, it made it difficult to change any system. It seemed as if no one was in charge with the ability to make change happen. An inner circle developed. These people knew the way government operated.

Therefore, their own interests became "the way." The good of the country was not even considered. Every move was made because of greed. Money and power were the reasons for all decisions.

Elected officials were chosen because of selected interest groups who spent money to get the person elected because he represented their cause. The free nation paid their leaders more than sufficient wages to do the work they were elected to do for their country. But the politicians had only their own interests and the interests of these groups of people with the money as the guide for their decision making.

Government contracts were awarded many times to people from these groups. Money was talking instead of people deciding what would be best for the whole country. *So many people were thinking only of themselves.*

Money was the center of all decisions. Everyone wanted a cut in this money. Everyone wanted the good life and there *seemed to be* no end to this money because government controlled the money supply.

Besides government contracts and programs, people also found out they could sue the government. Instead of an individual being responsible for his/her own actions, government made the institution instead of the individual responsible.

And yet, every person had to be careful that nothing *they* did could be misconstrued. Of course these rights to sue were even given to criminals. Life was becoming ridiculous. When people sued for damages, the amount of the award to the person who was suing became way too large and beyond even the use of common sense. Government money belonged to the taxpayers, yet juries awarded money as if there was no end to the supply. Many times the reasons for the lawsuits and these awards were ludicrous. Good judgement did not seem to enter into these decisions. Insurance money was also used because juries felt "insurance companies have lots of money." But it was all the people who contributed to the insurance company who supplied this money.

Welfare was also out of control. So many knew how to use the system. Fathers of children knew how to beat the system. They didn't take responsibility for their own children. Some parents were taking drugs. *How could parents who were taking drugs be responsible for their children? Was this one of the main reasons child abuse was growing? What could be done to help these children so they would not suffer from this unhealthy situation? Was public money used to buy illegal drugs and tickets to win money? Were these people good stewards of their money or did they use the children as their meal ticket for their own gratification?*

If public money was used, could laws have been passed to insure that this money was not used for anything other than its intended purpose? Maybe children should have been taken care of by someone else and these "parents" left to fend for themselves until they could be responsible for their children and society, who gave them the money in the first place.

Children were also taken advantage of in many ways. **To exploit or misuse children is the greatest crime against any society, and should have been treated as such.** And yet not many laws were passed to protect children or administer swift and effective penalties to the abuser. Abuse against children is one thing that society as a whole must stop if it wants future generations to have wholesome values.

Many people were talking and arguing for and against abortion. They couldn't come to an agreement but hardly anyone talked about preventing pregnancy in the first place. They only argued about when life began. Now they were saying that an embryo from conception on was no life, and at the same time they were growing these embryos in a dish and calling it life. They even went so far as to store this "unlife" for future use. People even had legal battles to determine who should have possession of this "unlife." Children are the most precious gift society has been given; yet, many were destroyed before birth. If there were no children, there would be no future society.

Few seemed to consider the right to life or the well-being of the "life" inside the woman. Yet, an induced miscarriage was an answer that many used, not prevention of pregnancy in the first place. This reduced the value given to human life.

Adequate education was lacking when it came to birth control measures. When pregnancy was prevented in the first place, an induced abortion was not necessary. Every time an abortion took place, life was destroyed. Pregnancy was a lifetime commitment; abortion was a minor inconvenience. It was argued that what a woman did with her own body was her right, but the fact remained that a life was destroyed and this "fact" was taken lightly by many. *Does anyone have the right to decide by themselves who can or cannot have life?*

CHAPTER IX - POLITICS

The president of the all-free nation was giving his yearly address. He was sniffing one of the many drugs available so he could get in touch with his inner self. He too couldn't kick the habit—it was firmly entrenched in his life. His "just say no" campaign clearly needed amending. His mistress was sitting discreetly in the front row of the rally applauding enthusiastically his plans for the disposal of nuclear waste residue.

The continental peoples' representatives dutifully and passively attended and listened to his speech. In their blissful ignorance they were enjoying the many favors they gave themselves.

The president was in charge of the country because the businessmen with the money had put him there. No longer were elections "necessary" because "their man" might not win.

With all the problems, his country was clearly in a mess. He had lost touch with reality long ago.

He never did understand the problems or had even noticed how poor his countrymen had become.

The streets were cluttered with garbage, needles and syringes. No one wanted to pick up this debris because everyone was afraid of the Affliction. Besides this—garbage collection had become too expensive. The Affliction had run rampant and was silently keeping its hold on society.

People were milling around—there was no work. They were hungry. They stood in line to collect the meager supplies the government supplied. It hadn't been many years ago when they had enough money to buy tickets to win money. Now all that money was gone too. The odds had never been in their favor, but they were willing to risk the little they had in hopes of winning.

Long ago, the businessmen had moved their factories to other countries. They were enjoying their wealth, discarding any responsibility to the free nation that enabled their business to begin.

Criminals controlled the cities. Everyone lived in fear. Because of their own free will, many people had rejected the rules of the Higher Power. Only their own self gratification mattered. Because of this, society was falling apart. The people who lived in a morally correct manner hid in their houses.

Even their children were exposed to this violence and corrupt living. In the countryside a few churches still existed but they were used for storage of government supplies. Any ordinary person did not have any more than his neighbor. He had found out long ago that his life and his family's would be in jeopardy if he had anything of value.

There were still places in the free land where people were leading the good life. They had purchased stock in the businessmen's factories that were built outside the free land—businesses that had left the country. They were still receiving their dividend checks. Their communities were kept safe by wire fences. These people heard stories of the life outside of their fences but it was not their responsibility if others had no money. But as time went on, even the people in the fences left the free land.

The military establishment was slowly controlling the country. Armed guards stood at the borders to continue to insure the country's freedoms. There had to be order. Someone had to be sure the government kept operating. Someone had to collect taxes. *The criminal joined the military. After all, who was better at insuring cooperation from the people?*

There was no trace of the peaceful existence they once had.

The checks and balances of this system had slipped too far in one direction. Individual "freedom" had survived, but not individual responsibility. There was disregard for the value of another person and his rights which were as important as their own rights. Individual freedom was given precedence over the good of the majority. The majority caused this to happen because they were not diligent in deciding what was best for society as a whole and let the individual rights supersede the rights of the majority. Rules did not have to be followed if the individual felt his freedom was violated. (Individuals were not responsible or accountable for their own actions. The system had been milked dry by individuals who made society monetarily responsible for their actions.) *This society was a blind society. While the people were allowing the morals of their country to disintegrate—democracy undid itself.* They let government become too centralized. Once this happened it was too hard to change any system.

Why was it so hard to keep government on the right track? Was change so subtle and difficult to interpret that people did not realize what was taking place until it was too late?

Standards had been the same from the time the free land was founded until toward the end of the latter years. Now there were no meaningful quality standards. A profit was made by any means. Smaller was packaged larger—the price was now increased. A dozen was changed to ten. Three pounds was thirty-nine ounces or less. There were no pennies.

Irresponsible government and credit card spending caused a debt in society that was almost impossible to repay.

The oceans were littering the seacoast with dead sea life and man-made debris which unthinking people had put there. *The ocean was large but even it couldn't cope with the damage man could cause with all his knowledge.* Too many fish and other sea life were taken, so even they couldn't reproduce to replenish themselves and each other. Their whole world was disrupted and hardly anyone noticed.

It was difficult to find a safe place anywhere in the *world.* Dictators were in power because the free nation (before their country made its major decline) didn't stand up strongly enough for human rights.

They professed freedom for all people, but at the same time supported dictators. This was because the all-free society felt they could not take over another country that they helped free from a dictator. The all-free nation left the little freed countries to begin again for themselves and choose their own leaders. This was an open invitation for another dictator to take over. If they, the all-free nation, as a society, ruled over another country, the very freedoms that they had for themselves would be denied the other country. *How could a nation succeed at freedom and liberty without someone to lead them?* There were always individuals or groups ready to control any society of people.

Responsible leadership with compassion would guarantee human rights for everyone, but not every leader was responsible or compassionate. A dictator who was only interested in power was a threat to all of society.

Now these dictators had weapons to destroy the earth. Each one was threatening to use it on each other. They were beginning to band together but it wouldn't be long before one of them would cause destruction so he would be all-powerful. The all-free nation had no say in this matter because their ability to make weapons of <u>protection</u> was gone. Long ago they cut back on weapons manufacturing because it was a way to save money for other uses. This would have brought about a better society if the money had been used for correcting the many problems their society had encountered. Instead the money never found its way to those people and projects for which it was intended. The money was mostly used to line the pockets of executives who were in charge.

The rules of the Higher Power were mostly forgotten. Some people were still trying to uphold these rules, but not enough people were willing to speak out and stand up for what was right.

The free people should have chosen leaders who really were concerned about their country and who looked toward the future.

It was a peacemaking effort to cut back on weapons manufacturing but at the same time the all-free people were not diligent in watching any dictator's potential weapons arsenal. They did not remain as strong as any potential aggressor. Now it wouldn't be long before an all-powerful leader would change their way of life.

All trace of their religion would vanish, control of the all-free people would become complete and there would be no love. *Could the all-free people who cherish their way of life still bring about change? Could good overcome evil? Did their disregard for the rules of the Higher Power cause the fabric of society to break down?*

WILL THE MORAL PEOPLE COME OUT OF THEIR HOUSES AND MAKE CHANGE HAPPEN BEFORE IT IS TOO LATE?

Epilogue

A dictator rose from within.
Business took over until finally
the country was destroyed.
Nature was pushed to its limit
and could no longer sustain life
as the all-free commanded.
Rules of the Higher Power
were mostly forgotten or ignored.
What life had been...

was never known again.